PRAISE FOR GIN

"Gina Kincade is imaginative, intelligent, and full of heart. It really takes a special writer to not only craft attention-grabbing, complex plots, but to also write three-dimensional characters that come alive on the page and in your hearts."

— Amazon Reviewer, TOP 100 REVIEWER

PRAISE FOR GINA KINCADE

The detailed descriptions of
everything from the storm to the
magical objects and spells brings
this whole new dynamic to the story,
enriching it, adding depth, bringing
to life every single part of the story,
no matter how big, small or even
how inconsequential it *may* seem.
It truly is What Lies Within Us that
makes this story the magical gem
that it is!
— *Cherri-Anne Boitson*, Leather &
Lace Reviews

PRAISE FOR GINA KINCADE

"Great storyline with characters that make the pages steam. Loved all the Christmas elements added into this spicy little tale. Do yourself a favor and gift yourself this story then, then put yourself on the naughty list by taking some time to indulge in this read."

— *Kirstein Howell, Vine Voice*

PRAISE FOR GINA KINCADE

"Having just spent the afternoon reading this wonderful book, I have to say that not only it is as captivating as it is sexy. The story moves along at a fast and furious pace taking you into a world of whirlwind romance and the paranormal. It kept me on the edge of my seat taking me into the story with every page."

— *Amazon Customer*

PRAISE FOR GINA KINCADE

This was a really fun, and hot, read. I spent most of the story grinning, heart pounding, eager for what would happen next. It's so great to see Gina writing again, as we're gifted with gems like On Santa's Naughty List. This story made me wish that I was in an area where we got a White Christmas, because it's perfect to warm you up on a cold winter's day.

I highly recommend it for anyone after some Christmas kink!

— Casey Kerwitz, Amazon Reviewer

HER FATED VAMPIRE

A VAMPIRE ROMANCE SHORT

HALLOWEEN STORY

COPYRIGHT © 2020 GINA KINCADE

ISBN: 978-1-77357-273-4

978-1-77357-186-7

978-1-77357-171-3

PUBLISHED BY NAUGHTY NIGHTS PRESS LLC

HTTP://NAUGHTYNIGHTSPRESS.COM/

COVER ART BY WILLSIN ROWE

Legal File Usage – Your Rights

TABLE OF CONTENTS

ABOUT HER FATED

VAMPIRE

There's no such thing as real vampires...right?

Carly Henderson thought attending a posh party at the home of her best friend's boss would be the same boring Halloween it had been for several years past. The last thing she expects is to spend a steamy night in an old crumbling castle. Apparently, though, things are not always as they appear, and it's going to be a night she will never forget.

Dominic Milani just made partner in his father's big law firm. To celebrate, he throws an elaborate Halloween party. Drawn inexplicably to the buxom brunette in the vampire costume, Nick may be in for more than he bargained for when he propositions her with the justification of 'just one night.'

Will Carly accept his secrets when Nick proves true that some

things are not always as they seem,
or is Nick destined to lose his fated
mate?

CHAPTER ONE

"SPENDING THE NIGHT in a creepy, crumbling down castle? How cliché. Ugh. I swear, if one more person tells me to loosen up, to have fun, to enjoy my life, I'm going to scream. No, seriously, I mean it," she grouched at the mirrored reflection she gazed at as she curled her hair.

"Yeah, go ahead. Call me extreme. I need to talk to myself right now. No one else really listens, anyway."

Running her fingers through the silky chocolate strands to even out the big curls, she paid special attention to the ones in front.

"Good enough," she spoke to the mirror again as she gave her hair one last glance and then added a light spritz of hair spray. "Tonight, I will give them *fun* and then some. Prove to everyone that I'm capable of having a good time, despite what they think. Of course, tomorrow I'll be as sick as a dog from too many drinks, I'm sure. But then I will go back to my life, my way! Why in the hell do I let them talk me into this shit?"

Really, can I help it if I'm just not often interested in their kind of fun?

UGH!

Just not my thing.

So sue me.

Once a year, Carly Henderson gave in to her friends' complaints that she never went out with them on their terms or their turf. It was true, they came to her or met her for dinner on the weekends at restaurants she liked, but she always turned them down when it came to loud parties and obnoxious bars.

But that was the point.

They did meet her on her terms. So once a year, the least she could do was meet them on theirs.

Right? It won't kill me.

Hasn't yet, anyway.

One or two drinks would be enough to get her raging drunk. She would probably make a fool out of herself, and whether she remembered it or not, her friends— who could down six beers and still recall every detail of the evening— would tell her all about it the next day. Through her hangover, she would moan and claim that she was done with the parties, their kind of nightlife. And they would remind her 'until next year.'

A vicious cycle.

Halloween night reared its ugly head once again, and she'd dutifully gotten dressed up in her costume.

Another deal.

Her friends took malicious delight in picking it out for her. Each year, they did the same shopping trip thing where she had to continually remind them she was in the room as they talked about her. Yes, maybe they should have all gone their separate ways long ago, but they had been her friends since grade school. Despite the fact they lived their adult lives differently, she loved them with all her heart.

Just not tonight.

As she slid the last bit of the skimpy costume over hips, she heard footsteps pound up to her apartment door. The girls' chattering and laughter got louder with each step.

A single knock, and they invaded the room. Shannon and Rebecca, her two best friends, all smiles, whistled like a pair of obnoxious males at her costume.

"I swear," Carly began, "I'm going to get arrested for indecent exposure on the way to this party in this get up. I mean, did they really make you pay for this thing? There is absolutely nothing to it!"

She admired her body in the mirror, the black corset did push up her boobs nicely, while the tight, black leather pants outlined the curves of her hips and thighs. She was a touch full-figured, but could still pull off the pants, especially given the crimson velvet cape she had flowing behind her. The black boots with nice high heels were her own addition, purchased a few years ago when her friends had put her in shoes that had given her numerous blisters and made her toes bleed by the end of the night.

Not forgetting that lesson anytime soon!

"You look hot, girl! The stores were good to us this year," Shannon spoke as she walked in a circle around Carly. "You make one smokin' hot vampire, bella."

"Yeah. Vampire. So original."

CHAPTER TWO

THEY CHATTED BACK and forth on the cab ride to the party. Living on the outskirts of LA meant every year the parties seemed to get more elaborate. Some big shot always tried to outdo the last big shot from the previous year. Tonight, her friends had already warned her that this was a party out a ways from the city, in an old, gated community of big houses. This one in particular, though, was in a castle.

Old money, mostly.

Shannon, who was the most outgoing of the three, had scored them the invites through a mutual friend at work. She was a legal intern at a pretty prestigious law firm.

"So, fill me in on this guy again," Carly tried to speak though her chattering teeth. They'd had to run through the cooling fall night air in order to catch the cab. It was supposed to be all of fifty-four degrees tonight and she'd felt the chill blast through the corset and cape as soon as they'd stepped out of her apartment. Even the warm cab didn't do the trick. The driver wore a coat, and had the temperature set to his preference, apparently.

So much for customer service.

Ugh.

When they finally rolled up to the large, decrepit looking castle at the end of the longest driveway inside the gated community, they couldn't help but stare appreciatively at the decked out arches and gardens surrounding the place. Ghosts hung from trees, while blinking orange lights highlighted the mock graves surrounding the walkway, complete with mummified remains smeared with some realistic looking blood.

Ewe. Gross.

They walked up the authentic wooden bridge to the door and Shannon handed three, gold-embossed invites to a stocky male bouncer in a tight black tee shirt and a pair of snug jeans.

Hmm. Yum.

"No costume necessary for him, I guess," Rebecca whispered in Carly's ear.

"The owner of the firm is out of town this weekend, so his son, who just made partner despite his age, is throwing the party this year. Nice guy. Ruthless in the court room, though. Cute and then some. Has an iffy rep with the ladies. But with all this money, I'm sure they are falling all over him. It's likely the ones he rejects who make up half the stories. If I see him, I'll be sure to introduce you, Carly," Shannon taunted with a wide smile on her face. Her nose all scrunched up made her look far younger than her twenty-five years.

The lady was a professional on the job through and through, but on the weekends, Shannon liked to cut loose. Her rep was worse than the boss' son by a long shot, but Shannon didn't care a bit. As she often told Carly, she was out to enjoy her life as long as she could.

She worked hard and deserved it—
all her words.

CHAPTER THREE

SEVERAL DANCES AND one drink later, Carly found herself abandoned by her friends who had already hooked up with some single guys from Shannon's firm.

She made her way through the crowded rooms to the bar for a diet soda now that she could get away with it. She already had a good alcohol buzz going. Well, maybe more of a mix of drink, thumping music, and thrashing her body about in the four-inch heels.

The inside of the house was nice, surprisingly all elaborate furnishings and expensive, if not totally modern decor. Just went to show that you couldn't judge a castle by it's outside appearance. Or was that a book by its cover.

Whatever.

She couldn't believe all the ghouls and goblins, adults mind you, drunk and in costume, lounging comfortably on the cream-colored suede couch. Of course, a couple practically screwed each other as they danced on the big recliner of the same color. But with this size house, and the money the family had, they could probably easily order a new living room set with one phone call.

She had to admit it made her somewhat uncomfortable to witness such grand displays of wealth. She hadn't grown up around it, so why should she think she could fit into it easily? This was not her world and she knew it

Sigh.

A dancing couple practically ran her down in the hallway. When they saw her come around the corner, they'd gotten more tied up in each other than they already had been, and the woman, dressed as a slutty angel or something along those lines with wings, started to fall. Mr. Motorcycle gang member, though you could tell with his crisp cut and businessman hair that it was definitely a costume, tried to catch her but they hit the floor in a tangle of limbs anyway.

Not before the winged lady's back hit the long, what looked like an antique cherry table, though. The contents on it shook, nearly toppling to the floor and Carly winced, jumping into action despite her towering heels.

Moving fast, she caught the half-filled glass of red wine someone had carelessly left sitting on the polished top. Instead of the burgundy liquid flowing onto the thick, cream colored carpet, she ended up splashing the remaining wine all over her chest as she went for a gilded picture frame that had started to fall. Still, despite the lush carpet covered floor, an old and expensive looking vase broke into pieces as she shivered from the horrible sensation of wine running between her breasts.

With all the noise the obviously drunk couple made, some weird noises between cries of pain and immature laughter, she hadn't heard anyone move up behind her.

"What the hell is going on in here?" A man's deep, loud voice rumbled, startling her. She spun around to find a man dressed in a vampire costume, looking rather annoyed at the mess now littering the hallway.

He helped the couple up, none too gently. Angel and motorcycle guy seemed to suddenly sober a bit, enough to make nice all over the man in the vampire costume, anyway. They apologized profusely, their hands all but brushing over the man's chest and back. He moved away as he said, "No big deal. Call yourselves a cab and call it a night, would ya?"

Carly couldn't help but laugh. "Sorry. I saved the wine glass and a picture, but just didn't have it in me to get the vase, too. Guessing this is your house?"

"It is, and I see I have another vamp here with me."

"Ah, yeah well, my girlfriends picked it out. You work with—or actually, Shannon, my girlfriend— she works for you. Or rather your father, I guess. Not sure how that works."

"My father made me a full partner. I just didn't want to add the 'and sons' bit to the name of the company yet. In fact, I didn't particularly see a need to change it at all. Just a minor detail, really."

"Oh. Well, that's great. Well, let me put these down and help you clean up this mess."

"Forget it," he said as glanced down at her wine-drizzled breasts.

Following his gaze, she realized her boobs had tried to make the great escape out of the corset from her sudden movements.

"Looks like you need to be cleaned up yourself."

"Yeah, when I went to grab the picture, the wine in the glass spilled all down the front of me. Who leaves an almost full glass of wine on a table in a hallway?"

"Bunch of adults, drunk and in costumes, I guess. Here, come with me while I get someone to pick up the glass, and we'll get you cleaned up as well. You look really soaked, and likely not very comfortable."

He touched the part of the corset hugging her stomach with his hand, the warmth of his palm going through the silk right to her skin.

"Sorry, uh, didn't mean to touch there. Just... How about I get you something else to wear, and get that dry-cleaned for you. It's the least I could do in exchange for you saving the glass and the picture of my grandparents."

"That's not..." she began, but he grabbed her hand and pulled her down the hall with him, waving her protests off with a motion of his other hand as they walked.

He moved them down the long hall to a door that swung open into a large kitchen. The room was so huge, with so many stainless steel appliances and white polished counter tops filled with every type of serving dish imaginable; it resembled the kind of kitchen found in a restaurant. The place literally buzzed with activity.

"Francis, would you get Margie, and tell her there is a broken vase down this hall. She is supposed to be working the rooms, so she might miss it."

"Yes, sir, Mr. Milani." This Francis person nodded, lowered the clipboard he had been writing on, and moved out of the kitchen at quite a rapid pace.

"Hmm, people jump at your command, huh, Mr. Milani?"

"I guess." He looked at her like she was from another planet for a moment until his gaze found her chest again. "Now, let's go get those beautiful breasts of yours washed up."

She jumped into action at his words. The thrilling zing his comment sent down through her belly, one that dampened her panties, gave her a boost of energy she'd thought lost on the dance floor.

His midnight black cape floated behind him, and she caught a glimpse at his tight black silk pants, which cupped nicely what looked to be a lusciously sculpted ass. Beyond this, his tight red shirt showed off every dip and valley of his six-pack abs. He had a firm hold on her hand, and his very presence seemed to demand not only her complete attention, but also her submission. With his dark, smoky eyes, jet-black hair and tanned features, the thought of being completely obedient to his every whim crossed her mind, and sent another rush of heated adrenaline to her already throbbing core.

Naughty girl. Stop those thoughts, right now!

You just met this guy.

Get your head in the game before you end up on the nightly news.

Nah. He's the son, partner, at a top law firm.

No way.

CHAPTER FOUR

SHE BARELY NOTICED how they had curved their way through the house, but butterflies warred with the electric lightning contractions swirling in her belly as they started down a steep flight of steps.

"You're taking me to the basement to clean up?" Her voice shook a little more than she would have liked, and she tugged backward on the hand he clutched in his, stalling a bit.

"Don't be scared now. This is my private lair. Vampire or not, this is my domain in the house and no one but me ever comes down here. I like how separate it is from the rest of the house, too. It's private, and I enjoy the seclusion. I made an agreement with my mother. If I didn't move out after college, which she preferred because she knew from my father's working hours how little she would see me anyway, then I could have the basement to myself. I insisted on getting it fixed up the way I like, and that only I would have a key."

"Nice—" She cut her words short as he unlocked the door and opened it to expose an expansive bachelor pad, the likes of which she had only ever seen on TV. Several couches, all a dark, coffee color leather, sat in a semi circle around a floor to ceiling entertainment center that went from practically one wall to the other.

The only exception that broke the expansive unit from the walls were two closed doors on either side of it. A softly lit bar ran the length of the back wall behind the sofas with just as many bar stools—looked to be ten in all—along the front of it. It was the same size as the one upstairs in the great room that she'd visited several times earlier that evening.

Artwork hung on the walls, sculptures sat in the corners, and each instance featured or represented naked people in some sort of sexual act.

Um.

Wow.

She knew she stared at the depictions of male anatomy in all shapes and sizes in coupled positions with voluptuous, nude females in the throes of passion, but she couldn't pull her gaze away as she wondered if she'd just stepped into a perilous den of inequity.

Gulp.

"You appreciate the artwork, then?" he asked, a smug half-smile on his face, his eyes sparkling despite the low light in the room. The only additional lighting available to them, other than that over the bar, came from flickering electric candles hung on the walls to the sides of the doors.

She hoped the heat that had risen up her neck and face couldn't be seen in the surroundings. "Yes, I guess. A bit...a...well, more wanton than I'm used to seeing. The whole place is a bit gothic, really. This isn't the part where you tell me you are a real vampire and drink me dry, is it?"

His deep gravely laugh rang out loud and echoed throughout the room. "Halloween getting to you? But I will warn you, I *am* a bit of a beast. That is, if you're interested. To date, though, every woman who has entered my lair has walked out of here alive, all of her blood still running through her veins."

"Interested?" she asked, not really of him, but more of herself. This was her one night to cut loose, yes, but never in all her years had she been propositioned with such a terrifying and thrilling offer such as this one. Usually she just got drunk, felt up on the dance floor by a handsy drunk guy or two, if she was lucky, and then driven home. Of course, she wasn't exactly sure what he was offering her at the moment, but he *had* said everyone survived it. Yeah, you could call her interested. Out of everyone at the party, he stood as the one too hot opportunity to let herself enjoy the night in a whole new way.

Why not?

What have you got to lose?

CHAPTER FIVE

HE GAVE A gentle tug on her hand, leading her through the closest of the two doors on the back wall and interrupting her internal conversation. He pulled her through a bedroom, and then into a bathroom too huge to describe. The room came fully equipped with a Jacuzzi tub, sauna, shower and all.

Holy shit!

"I swear, this basement is four times the size of my apartment," her thoughts came out of her mouth before she could stop them. She slapped a hand over her mouth, eyes wide as heat crept up her neck and filled her cheeks.

He chuckled. "It's under a big house. Now, let's get these wet clothes off you and get you cleaned up." Before he even finished his sentence, he had pulled on the laces of her corset and her breasts spilled out.

"Wow, I could have done that myself, thank you," she spat out, more surprised than anything as she slapped her arms across her chest, covering herself.

"Don't do that," he commanded in his authoritative voice, his brows drawn down over dark, glittering eyes. "Allow me to assist you. "

"I can wash myself."

"I'm sure of that," he countered, his gaze running over her body. "But now that you're here, I would like to propose something a little bit more to both of our tastes."

"Go on." She was intrigued despite herself.

"You will allow me to clean you and, after, you will accompany me for a night of pleasure."

Oh my god!

Whoa!

"Well, that was direct," she spat back at him, her shock making her tongue loose.

"Yes, I am. I won't apologize for it either. Yes or no?"

"What exactly am I committing to? Just a bath, or also to you and I in that bed built for four out there?"

"No. I never share my bed. The other room, the other door, is my room for all sexual activities. Safe word provided."

Um...what?

Her heart dropped, but her body reacted. Her panties were definitely soaked now and her nipples were sharp points under her palms. "Uh, sorry. I may have agreed to the sex," she stumbled over the words. Then she mumbled to the side, "this was supposed to be my one night of abandon this year, but—" she left off as she looked back up into his dark sexy eyes; ones that really seemed to glow in the low light—like a vampire's might. That last thought hovered on her mind for a moment before she pushed it away.

Yeah, she would have agreed to the sex, but who the hell knew what was in that other room.

"Never submitted to a man, then?"

"What are we talking about here? Submit how? Sexually? As in, domination?"

"Just some fun. Yes. I like women to do as I say, give in to my every desire, no matter how depraved I'm feeling at the moment. The safe word is just in case I start to go past the level you are comfortable with. "You're a virgin?"

"No."

God.

Of course not.

"Have you ever explored anything other than normal vanilla encounters?”

Oh wow.

Um...

She gulped and then shook her head as she tried to catch her breath, her heart thumping loud enough in her chest she was sure he could hear it.

The idea of truly letting go, all the way, of trying something so out of her comfort zone it wasn't even funny, thrilled something deep inside her. She shivered, longing to give in to his request, no matter how much it also scared her. Could she do it? Even on this one night of the year, this was far more than she'd planned, maybe more than she could handle.

What if she freaked out?

What if he did?

"I'm in a mellow mood tonight. Give it a try. The minute you are uncomfortable in any way, with anything, you say 'Mr. Milani.' That puts me right into work mode. Kills the mood in a heartbeat. So, a safe word at its best. Otherwise, from here on in, you would call me only Sir."

Huh.

"Sir, really? This is how you get off?"

"Yes. Take the offer or leave it."

She tried to figure out where she stood on this whole matter. Seriously, this night each year she played at being someone she wasn't. This situation presented as a bit extreme, but there was a safe word and all. Hell, she could say it three minutes from now, or not at all. She had no idea what she was in for, but something inside her clicked.

Go for it!

"I'll take it," came from her mouth in a quick rush of words.

"I'll take it, Sir."

"I'll take it, Sir," she parroted back in a small voice. Her nipples tightened further under her hands, if that were even possible, and heat rushed to her core.

"Then move your arms," he growled out, the command clear that he expected to be obeyed.

She complied, dropping her arms to her side as her blood rushed through her veins.

He went right back to work, unlacing her corset like a pro. Her slick sex literally pulsed as she stood there, arms practically clamped to her sides, as this man undressed her, enjoyed the view of her body with no shame. Her cape fell to the floor at the same time as her corset.

"Mmmm. Beautiful." His eyes glittered as he brought his hands up to brush his thumbs over her already aching nipples.

"Am I allowed to speak freely, Sir?" She panted, her breaths coming rapidly as he caressed each breast in turn as if he'd just exposed a delicious meal he couldn't wait to bite into.

"You are, as long as you address me properly. You will profit from it in the end." He winked and stepped back. "Remove the rest yourself."

"Yes, Sir," she answered, missing the heat of his hands on her already. She licked her lips, realizing she became all hot and bothered by his directness, his curt tone, and his commanding ways. It made no sense to her whatsoever.

She was a basic hermit who loved her independence, but she went with it. Again, tonight would be all about being someone she wasn't, she reminded herself. Only thing was, at this point, she already feared she may like it all a little too much in the end.

He watched her closely, dark eyes roving over her body as she undressed.

She wiggled the boots off her feet. Never before had she thought of how her boobs swayed as she did now with his penetrating gaze making her aware of every nuance, every movement of her body.

Usually her shoes were the first things to go.

"Stay," he commanded with his hand up, his palm facing her like she was a dog.

Yet, rather than be offended, once again she said, "Yes, Sir." Her voice had become breathier each time she spoke, to the point now that it hardly sounded like her.

She stood there, didn't dare move a muscle while he ran the bath water. Sticky from the wine, watching the steam rise off the water, she couldn't wait to share the tub with him. The thing was big enough for four, at least, with seats on one side.

"Come here," he barked, and she jumped.

Yet, she played her role and obeyed enthusiastically.

Maybe too willingly.

When she moved to the tub and stood still beside him, he said in a flat tone, "Bend over, hands on the tub, legs spread wide apart for my inspection."

Oh my!

"Uh, yes, Sir." She did as he asked. For the second time tonight, she felt uncomfortable but aroused all the more. Once she was in position, she could feel the heat of him. He was so close, yet he didn't touch her. Instead, she felt his warm breath on her thighs, on her hidden places, then on her ass.

She wanted to wiggle her hips, beg for him to touch her, but she remained frozen, as he wanted her to be, and felt damn proud of herself for accomplishing the feat. Seconds later, though, she yelped when his fingers ran over her slick, heated folds.

"Nice and wet, I see. You do want this," he said as he forced one finger roughly up inside her and then pulled it back out just as quick.

Her inner muscles grabbed for him, but were too late. So, empty instead, she throbbed.

She whimpered, then followed with, "Sorry, Sir." But, she had no idea why.

"No apologies. You may react to my touch or whatever else I do to your body. I like the sounds; they are real. I'm not a Dom, if that is what you think. I am just a dominant personality, who likes to take what I want, even if I demand to be the submissive. My sexual preferences change with my moods, but know I do always like to hear my women admit their pleasure, if in a whimper, a sigh, or a scream. No one can hear us down here."

He said the last part in her ear in nothing but a whisper, sending a chill racing down her spine.

"Shit, I am going to love working this ass," he said as he grabbed her butt cheeks. He wasn't gentle, but tonight, she didn't mind. In this place, she wanted it hard and rough. Maybe she had costumed her way into a new personality tonight. And maybe she would like it so much she would have to apologize to her friends forever grumping about her one night out a year.

He spread the mounds of her ass apart, and licked over her puckered hole. "Has anyone ever taken you here?"

"No, Sir." She breathed through the sensations shooting into her stomach, into her trembling pussy. The ones that made her want to fuck him, hard, wild, with an abandon she'd never allowed herself before.

"An ass virgin, well then, this shall be fun. Get in the tub, now," he commanded.

As she stepped into the water, she noted that it was almost a little too hot, enough that it brought a sting to her skin. "Are you going to join me, Sir?" she asked.

"No. I'll watch, sometimes help. Actually, let me start you off by soaping your breasts. I can at least take the wine off you. Here, sit up on the seat. I'll start the jets."

"Thank you, Sir." She sighed as the water shot at her back, her legs, and her arms. It felt so good, so luxurious. To top off the moment, he soaped his bare hands and started to wash her breasts. Just as he had been so far, he was abrasive. The circles he scrubbed over her flesh went hard and fast. Her nipples pebbled under his hands, begged for more attention than just his palms rubbing over them.

When he pulled away, he said, "Now, I want you to spread those legs as wide apart as they will go and work your clit until you come for me." His voice this time, carried more of the lighter tone of a request rather than a command.

Doing as he said, she was shocked to the point of letting out a little yelp at how sensitive her clit was, how swollen. All of this play, whatever he called it, had gotten her a step beyond excited to the point she would just about do anything for some kind of release.

With his gaze directed between her legs as he leaned against the side of the tub, it took very little to throw her over the edge. She moaned when the tiny pulses of electricity in her clit took on the sensation of heat washing over her. Yet, it was short lived, and somewhat of a letdown. She wanted more, and she wanted it by his hands.

CHAPTER SIX

"YOU LOOK LIKE a hungry woman, one with sexual needs. You are exactly where I wanted you. Now, let's get you dried off and into the dungeon."

Dungeon?

"Yes, Sir." Just thinking the word made her inner walls clench. Maybe there was more to her than even she'd dreamed. Of course, with boyfriends few and far between because she rarely went out, she hadn't let herself dream much. A dildo, a good picture of a naked man in her mind, and she was pretty much good to go.

In just a towel, she tiptoed the short walk to his so-called dungeon, which did not by any means resemble the word once they got in there. He flipped a light switch and, oddly, all it turned on were a few dim lamp lights. The furnishings sat a bit more rustic. He did have two candelabras as tall as her, and he lit each of all the eight candles in them. There were two wooden chairs; nothing special about them other than one of them had four handcuffs hanging from it, two on the front legs and two on the back rungs. Something that looked like a balance beam sat between them. Again, the wooden legs sported cuffs. As well, some kind of shackles hung on the wall. A very plush looking animal skin carpet laid to one side on the floor in front of a low unit of shelves filled with sex toys, bottles she assumed to be lubricant, and other implements she recognized, like a whip and a paddle.

She tensed up as she wondered just how this would all feel.

Will it hurt?

Will I be able to take it?

Will I like it?

Shit, what if I like it?

What will that say about me?

Her ass clenched as butterflies beat inside her stomach.

Are they anxious and excited, or merely afraid?

"What is your safe word?" he asked as he came up behind her. "Whisper it like it's a bad word." He had long ago taken out his set of fake vampire teeth, and ditched his cape, so he looked good enough to eat.

"Mr. Milani, Sir," she hissed as quietly as she could manage.

"Thank you. Shall we begin?"

"Yes, Sir." A shudder went through her, the wetness between her legs, still a bit damp from her bath, started to get thicker. Oh, was she ever ready, and it couldn't have shocked the hell out of her more.

Just then, she heard her phone ring in the other room where it had been pinned into the waistband of her leather pants.

"Get that."

She nodded before she took off, naked, back for the other room. She was in a definite hurry for more reasons than one.

"Hello," she said breathlessly.

"Carly, where the hell have you gotten off to? We can't find you anywhere up here."

"I'm here. In the house."

"Well, that was purposefully vague. Anyway, Rebecca is already gone, caught a cab with some guy from my office. I'm about to take off myself. Are you going to be okay to get a cab home?"

"Sure, no problem. Won't be the first time, right?"

"Funny. So who are you with and where are you, girl? In a bedroom somewhere?"

"Something like that. Tell you later. I gotta go."

"Holy shit! I like the sound of that, girl! Call ya tomorrow, and I want every detail!"

That was the last she heard before she clicked the phone off.

CHAPTER SEVEN

HEADING BACK TOWARD the dungeon, she craved a few details herself.

"So, while you were on the phone, I was considering where I want you first. Actually, I think I want your cape back on, and a few other things. Tonight, this is a vampire's lair instead of a dungeon."

Surprised, she noticed that both of their capes dangled from his fingers, as well as both of their sets of fake teeth. Her boots lounged at his feet.

"When did you grab those...ah, Sir?"

"I'm quick and quiet. Besides, I wanted to eavesdrop on the phone conversation to make sure nothing would ruin our evening."

"But, you said you were not a real vampire," she laughed a bit; the idea of a vampire was just in the television shows, right?

Yeah, right.

No Vampire Diaries for me.

Damon Salvatore...

Sigh.

She chuckled again, to herself this time, at the ridiculousness of the thought.

Quick.

Quiet.

Good hearing.

All vampire traits.

Her imagination was as vibrant as ever, it seemed.

Especially tonight.

"Put these on." He handed her cape to her, and she slung it on over her nude body. "These, too." She reached for her boots and slipped them back on as well. She oddly felt even more naked with only the cape and boots on.

Then, he slid her fake teeth into her mouth, fitting the plastic snuggly over her real teeth. She thought she might prefer a gag. These things just made you slobber all over yourself.

He did the same with his own set of fake teeth, completing his costume, and he looked damn sexy in a dark and sinister kind of way.

Without saying a word, he took her arm and led her to the wall. He lightly pushed her back against it. First he clasped her hands into the shackles above her head. This moved her cape back so it framed her body but hid nothing from his dark, sultry gaze. Then, he separated her feet and locked the shackles on around the ankles of her boots. The distance between her feet made her strain to stay upright in her heels.

"You are devilishly sexy right now. He ran his fingers lightly over her breasts, down her stomach, and then trailed the tips through the small patch of hair on her mound. She trembled, wanting him, needing him inside her. But, she was well aware that was far off, as he still stood fully clothed, and there was a lot of stuff, infinite possibilities, in this room, of things to be done to her.

When he grabbed a thick candle from the shelf and lit it from one of the tall candelabras, she became perplexed as well as a tad nervous. A cold sweat broke out on the back of her neck under her cape.

What the...?

He held the taper over her breasts first, but high in the air. She held her breath as he tipped the thick wax form, let just a tiny drizzle of wax fall on the skin just above her breasts. She sucked in her breath at the tiny burn and then it was gone. Though not much wax actually dropped from the candle, she somehow knew this one had to be made from that special paraffin wax they used in candles made for this sort of thing.

Thank God.

She relaxed, back straight against the wall, a tiny bit more at ease.

Oh wow.

Oh...

He continued to do the same, little dribbles of hot wax, over her stomach and on her thighs. None of the burns made her yell out in pain, but she found they set her nerves to tingling all over her body, inside and out.

She squirmed a bit against the wall, wanting him more now. She needed something large up inside her in the worst way—a way that she would do anything to achieve right now.

Take me, now.

I need, I want...

Ugh.

"I see someone wants some relief from her body's needs. Here, let's see if this works for you."

He walked over to the shelves, blew out the candle and cut off the wick with a pair of tiny scissors. Rubbing the wet wax with his fingertip, his teeth clenched tight together, he covered over the spot where the wick had been. Then he picked the wax off his skin.

"Kiss it," he said as he held up what had been his wax-coated finger. The skin at the tip of his digit looked an angry red, but not blistered or anything.

Huh.

He doesn't burn?

Aren't vampire's impervious to fire?

She shook her head, banishing the thoughts of vampires and did as she was told. It just wasn't anywhere near her best work with her plastic vampire teeth in.

However, he appeared amused.

He used the candle to play over her nipples first, which were so sensitive and tight the solid of the candle brought about sensations of pleasure that bordered on pain. Want, pure and primal, made her shift her hips, thrust her mound out toward him. Playing with her nipples became all about the need of her sex, each pulse of the nerves shot straight to her core.

"Yes, I know where you want this," he murmured.

It's nothing more than a dildo, she had to reassure herself there for a minute. Yet, when the smooth wax moved between her wet folds, all she could do was close her eyes and get lost in the feeling as it slowly slide up inside her. He moved it in and out while he twisted it, making the fat taper hit each part of her soft, soaked inner flesh.

She thrust her hips, but he stopped them with his hand, pressed her hard against the wall. She cried out, her body demanding a nice thick cock inside her so badly she could barely breathe. Sweat glistened on her face as she began to pant.

"I think you want too much. Let's see how much further we can take you, though."

CHAPTER EIGHT

SHE WAS GRATEFUL when he unhooked her from the wall as her legs had begun to shake to the point she no longer felt they would support her, especially in her blessed boots.

She stumbled as he led her to the chair with restraints. He hooked her into it; her thighs wide open as they stretched to straddle it, to be locked to the sides of the legs.

Her breasts jutted out as he hooked her arms to the sides of the backrest. So wanton, so needy, so pleased at the same time with him and herself for withstanding everything so far.

She relaxed against the wood, even welcomed the way it pushed against her body. She had become all about *more* here.

Soon, he threw aside the candle, and grabbed a large vibrator from the shelf. With her head hanging to the side, she could see him smile.

She shook with desire; the thing was larger, wider, and longer than any dildo, or man, she had ever known.

Instead of using the other chair as she thought he would, he sat on the floor in front of her. With his fingers, he opened her slick folds, and leaned down to press his heated mouth over her clit, then trailed kisses and licks down over her overly sensitized skin.

Her ass practically bounced on the seat as she tried to get more of his mouth on her.

He licked over her labia, lapped up her wetness, and then latched onto her clit. He sucked hard, tongue flicking over her swollen bud, until she came once more.

Holy shit!

"Sir, I need something inside me. Please," she choked out, her insides never having wanted, needed release this much.

He took the vibrator and shoved it up inside her slick channel, fast and hard. She gasped, but welcomed the broad intrusion. The glorious feeling of being spread so wide was beyond wonderful, and she started to fuck the thing instantly, bucking her hips, looking for some relief from the heat burning within her core.

When he pulled it out of her suddenly, she could feel the pricks of tear in her eyes. "No!" she cried out.

"My dear, you can not tell me *no*. That is a forbidden and punishable act! You will learn to be grateful for the pleasure I provide, and patiently wait for what *you* want."

To say 'sorry' was on the tip of her tongue, but then he stood and opened his pants and out popped his erection, quickly diverting her attention from the apology. His cock rivaled the size of the fake one that had just been inside her.

Holy shit.

No wonder he uses one that size, it's to prepare the woman for what's to come.

Hot damn, but how she wanted it, too.

"Suck me," he commanded, his voice back to being low, fierce, raspy with his teeth still in.

He pulled her fake teeth out, and pushed his cock into her willing mouth. Moving himself, grasping her hair in one fist and his cock in the other, he fucked her mouth until her cheeks ached.

He drew himself from her salivating mouth, tucking his hardness back inside his pants, and she felt the loss intensely, wanting to feel him throbbing against the back of her throat some more. She'd never been so interested in giving head as she was at that moment. It became a need, a desire to please him more.

CHAPTER NINE

MR. MILANI BENT AT the waist, and unlocking the four cuffs, he pulled her up from the chair, supporting her body like she was nothing but a rag doll.

He grasped her by her arms, near dragging her across the room, not that she resisted his force at all. With a firm hand on her back, he then bent her over the balance beam sort of thing. This time her arms and legs were spread to the sides and clamped into place with shackles on the feet of the thing.

Now, more than before, ass up, she hung very exposed, especially since he had pushed her cape to one side after he had secured her.

Groan.

The position embarrassed her but yet at the same time she felt a renewed rush of wetness to her core, anticipating, wondering what he planned for her next.

When he moved to the shelves, she lifted her head, curious to see what toys the man grabbed. Even though she wanted to be filled too much to care what came next at this point, she still wanted to know what was coming.

He picked up a little rubber black thing.

A butt plug.

Although she'd never owned one, she was familiar from sex toy shopping one time with Shannon and Rebecca. Ass, pussy, she was just too needy to care at the moment. She thought she would be more afraid, but she was actually welcoming the new experience, curious, desperate for relief.

After he lubed it up, he came over to stand behind her.

"Relax," he demanded, his hand now caressing over her exposed ass. She didn't need to spread herself open, but he pulled one cheek a little more to the side with his steely grip.

She felt his tongue first, which shocked her, sent her pussy to throbbing overtime, trickling more of her heated juices between her already drenched lips. He licked over her puckered hole several times, made her squirm and moan before he bit her ass cheek lightly.

She cried out, but the noise soon stopped when she felt the plug at her opening. She felt too tight to let it in, but he commanded, "Relax and push out onto the plug, my dear."

She did as he instructed and the plug slipped in about half an inch. An electric current started in her ass and went right through her sex. In fact, now she could feel her own wetness no longer trickling but actually flowing out of her throbbing channel and coating her thighs.

He slowly, methodically pushed the butt plug a little more into her ass, and then a little more, until the pain, the burn of it, gave way to a blessed tremor of bliss, fullness.

"Mmmm, you like that. I can tell by the little wiggle and shake of your tight ass and the additional juices flowing from you. Maybe one day we could train you to the point of letting my cock in your tight, fine ass."

Oh my god.

Yes!

"Maybe, Sir," she answered. She found it unbelievable that he spoke about the future when she had prepared herself for just a one-night stand.

Was this more than just tonight?

Could I do that?

Would I want that?

Of course!

This man was a master. Never had she wanted more, so much, so fast.

"Maybe?" His hand came down on her ass with a smart sounding smack, igniting a stinging burn on her right cheek. Only, when she tensed, the inner wall of her anus bore down on the plug, made her pussy clench. If she moved just right, she could see his erection bob with his movements.

On the way to affix her to this contraption, he had taken off his shirt as well. But, from her angle she could only catch a glimpse of his six-pack abs. Even then, they were a lean, fit type of sexy.

"I just didn't know you wanted more, Sir. Well, more than tonight."

"I do. There is something about you... You are so willing, yet so naive. You are beautiful, and I want to know more about you. I want to know how far you can go..." he left off.

Oh my.

Wow.

More...

She couldn't think of anything to say in response. Another group of butterflies took to flight in her stomach. He unhooked her, and she wondered briefly if he had meant to do more there.

When he eased her body up, he reached under her legs and lifted her up, cradling her against his firm, bare chest. He looked serious, like he had something to say, but held his mouth in a tight grimace. When he looked as if he was going to kiss her mouth, he gave her a peck on her forehead instead.

Um...

What the?

She didn't know what to make of any of it.

CHAPTER TEN

MR. MILANI WALKED to the chair and sat down on it, placing her on her feet beside him.

"I've changed my mind. I want you over my knee. I need to spank you. I want to feel your delicious dripping slit on my thigh with each smack." His voice was gravely with a hint of sadness, and she wondered if she'd done something horribly wrong.

She wasn't given time to consider it, or even ask as he pulled her down over his knee, spread her thighs apart, and took to spanking her ass with his bare hand; hard, one cheek then the other.

Her ass was on fire, and she squirmed over the rough fabric of his pants, wanting to feel his hardness against her belly and practically falling off his lap in the process. Shamelessly, she begged for more.

Who knew this could turn me on so much?

Pulling the butt plug from her roughly and tossing it in the direction of the shelves, he laid more centered smacks on her burning ass, one after another. She screamed out a few times, but didn't ask him to stop.

She didn't want to stop.

"You have a safe word if you need it," he hissed at her.

He was like a man possessed with punishing her, and she loved every minute of the pain, which felt oh, so good. But, just when the burn started to win, just when she thought she might actually have to use her safe word, he stopped, slid to the floor, and pulled her to his lap. Tears stung her eyes, but he kissed them away before they could fall.

"I want you," he breathed heavily.

"I know, Sir. You have me."

"No, that is not what I mean. I want you in a way I don't know what to do with. Ever since I saw you upstairs, I have wanted nothing more than to take you to my bed. And, as I said, I invite no one there. All of this, it was some kind of test, I guess. Of me, of you... I don't know what has come over me. My father speaks all the time of love at first sight, fated mates and all that, and I never put any stock in it. I like sex. I like it rough, and...well, you never once complained, though I feel you have never experienced anything like what I have asked of you. But tonight, though great so far, it isn't exactly what I wanted. Will you share my bed?"

Love?

Fated mates?

What was he going on about?

"Yes, Sir."

"No, call me Dominic. Nick."

"Are you sure?"

"I am, Carly. I want you in my bed more than anything I have ever wanted in my life. Just you, skin against skin, I want to make love to you. Trust, in years to come, I'm going to want to experiment with you more and more, push your body, see all it can endure, see all it wants, give you pleasure in every way available to us both. But right now, will you grant me a first? Come to my bed?"

Oh wow!

She nodded, her mind spinning and so many emotions hitting her all at once. It was all she could do. She wanted everything he'd mentioned just as much as he did.

God, help me.

CHAPTER ELEVEN

AS HE FOLLOWED her down onto the soft mattress in the moonlit bedroom, Nick's lips brushed over the pulse at the base of her throat and she could almost swear she felt the sting of something sharp graze over her tender skin.

"God, Carly, I have never wanted anyone so much. You have me enthralled in some spell, I'm sure." He nuzzled his nose in the hollow of her neck and shoulder and sucked in an audible breath.

She chuckled and tilted her head back to give him more access to her throat. "Sorry, not a witch." She could feel the outline of his hardness pressing through his snug slacks and into her belly, leaving no doubt whatsoever of his desire for her, and it set her mind reeling.

"Maybe not a witch, but definitely a seductress... Succubus? Siren?" She watched his eyes flash light as he raised his head to stare into her eyes.

"Nope, sorry. Nothing supernatural here. Just plain human."

"There's nothing plain about you, Carly." His eyes resumed the darkened, lust-filled stare and he licked his lips. "You are enchanting, and I can't wait to feel myself deep in your heat, hear you as you scream my name. Sink my teeth into your..." Nick groaned long and deep in his throat, almost like he was in pain. Or growling.

"Yes, please." Carly bucked her hips, eager to feel his hardness within her pulsing channel.

Nick pulled up from her for what seemed like a spilt second, divesting himself of his pants and finally freeing his erection from the confines of the material. She gave little thought to how fast he appeared to move, more interested in his velvet-over-steel pale member that greeted her gaze in the moonlight and caused her mouth to salivate once more.

Another time she'd have more of him, make a meal out of his cock like she wanted to. Perhaps make that sexy growl bubble up from his throat some more.

She giggled inwardly, pushing the thought to the back of her mind and raising her arms to welcome Nick as he hovered over her, his hips fitting between hers and his hardness pressing against her thigh.

Nick shook his head before bringing his mouth to her lips, kissing her again, this time gentle brushes of his lips against hers, his hands moving through her thick hair and sending shivers down her spine.

"I want you in the worst way, Carly," he said in a choked voice, his breathing staccato, punctuated by each press of his lips over her chest, tracing a heated path down her jaw to the hollow at the base of her throat, moving to each of her breasts, nibbling on her pebbled pink nipples.

The heat built between them, coupled with a deep ache in her core. She needed him to take her, fill her, own her. The last thought scared her but she pushed the apprehension away and pressed her hips upward. "I want you too, Nick. So much."

Nick pulled back once more, leaving her feeling bereft after the heat of his kisses. "My only fear right now is how we do this after tonight. You've captured me. I didn't believe it true before, that it could actually happen... I never understood what my father was talking about. You know, what it'd feel like, how everyone always says, 'when you meet her, you will just know,' but, even if we have no future, if that's not what you want after tonight, I will at least have this night with you. Something I will cherish for the rest of my days. Although, that is not all I want. Not by a long shot."

She shook her head. "I can't think through all of that right now, Nick. For now, just make love to me tonight. I want it, too. I want this with you. Let's deal with the tomorrows later, okay," she whispered, her mouth roving over the cool skin of his shoulder, his neck, pausing over his firm chest for a few breaths, trying to calm the pounding of her heart and her own erratic breathing.

She gripped the sheets, writhing beneath him. "Take me now. Make me yours just for tonight. Let me feel you inside me, Nick. I can't wait anymore!" She groaned, bringing her teeth down over his pearled nipple. "And, please, don't be gentle. I won't break."

Nick growled and dived down to graze his teeth over her throat once more. "Yes, m'lady. Your wish is my command."

He notched his cock at her entrance. Then, grasping her hips in his hands, pulling her upward to meet him, with a quick thrust, he was inside her, balls deep. The stretch and burn as she accommodated him in her tight sheath felt like a welcome relief to the ache that had built before.

"So tight. So warm." He withdrew and plunged deep again.

"Nick... I..." She needed more. She grabbed for his ass, digging her fingers into the pale globes.

"Am I hurting you?"

"Only in the best way." She wrapped her legs around his hips, pulling him to her.

Her stomach tightened and her legs trembled as he thrust in and out in a quicker rhythm until he took her up and over that edge, made her scream his name, even as he growled hers.

Her hips bucked with him, moving in a rushed synchronicity as she rode out the overwhelming contractions, the ripples of pain and pleasure that destroyed her mind, turned her body to pure heat and nothing else as she felt him let go deep within her.

Spent, he moved to the side of her, pulling her into his arms and cradling her to his body. "You've just given me one of the best nights of my life," he said, stroking the chocolate locks of her hair and pressing a gentle kiss to her forehead. "Tomorrow. We will find a way."

Her bones feeling like jelly, she fell asleep with a smile on her lips, happier than she ever thought possible.

EPILOGUE

One year later...

CARLY TIED THE cape around her shoulders and then smoothed her hands over the blood red corset and down the front of the black leather pants. In the mirror, she watched as

Nick slid into his matching black leather pants and damn near drooled at the image he presented. All tight ass, six-pack abs framed by a red silk shirt, and silky dark hair topping the most gorgeous face she'd ever laid eyes on.

Yeah, she was undeniably in love.

Sigh.

Tugging her hair to the side, she ran a fingertip over the lightly raised skin there. Today was the one year anniversary of the day they met. The day everything in her world changed for the better. The Halloween party at an old and crumbling castle had given her so much more than she could've ever dreamed of having in this lifetime.

Who in their right mind would ever have guessed Nick and his family were real vampires. All the commercialized nonsense of their inability to walk in sunlight, cold skin, no heartbeat... Well, she'd learned the truth. Okay, the sunlight bit was partly true. They wore a charm, typically a bracelet or ring, to protect them from the blistering rays and allow them outside whenever.

Though Nick had worried she'd reject him in her fear of the unknown, Carly's life long fascination with the supernatural, in particularly vampires, had apparently prepared her for the man—no, vampire—that she was destined to spend the rest of her life with.

Nick was no Damon Salvatore, but he was her own personal Dominic Milani and she'd decided that fact over fiction was better any day.

Who knew a simple party would bring her face to face with her fated vampire.

The End

* * *

Enjoyed this short story?

Be sure to check out more of my books on select retailers!

All my links are at the end of this book for your convenience.

Have a great one!

**Turn the page for a sizzling hot
taste of another of my books!**

EXCERPT

Read a preview of my Holiday story, Mistle Tie Me, Book 1 in the Shifting Hearts Dating App series, co-written with the amazing Erzabet Bishop...

Demi   watched   the   bartender

perform his antics behind the bar and turned back to Nick.

An armored bear with no armor. Interesting.

But now he'd gotten it back because someone had fallen in love with him. Did he mean her?

She blinked, considering the crazy events of the evening. Love? It was a little too soon for that, but she decided she liked being in Nick's company. And he filled out his leathers like a man who knew what he was about.

A grin spread across her face. She wanted to stay longer and see Hades ground under Persephone's boot. It appeared, to her great surprise, that her daughter had things well in hand.

Oh. Right. Nick had asked her out for coffee.

"I might be persuaded." Demi looked out over the leather clad people and shook her head. She paused, scanning the room and searching for her daughter and Rhoda once more.

She'd never met a man she wanted to see dragged around by his neck more than Hades. The jerk had it coming. Part of her wondered what he'd done to piss off her daughter. Then she decided she didn't want to know.

No.

They had their own lives to lead.

Maybe it was time for her to do the same.

She eyed the man in front of her and considered her options. There was something wild about him and she wanted to explore that.

"Let's go." Nick held out his hand, eyes twinkling in the strobes and light show. He frowned, noting her hesitation. "Or do you need to wait for your friend?"

Her gaze met his. She held out her hand. "No. She's probably found her plaything for the night."

He laughed, pulling her away from the wall. "Come on. It only gets rowdier the later it gets."

"I'll bet." Demi brushed a bit of Underworld off her skirt. "Let's go."

"What do you want to do first?" He brushed his fingers along her cheek and lowered his lips to hers.

Demi broke the kiss and stepped away.

Did she want that?

Did she want him?

Gray eyes smoldered back at her and she lost some of her resolve to leave. The pulse of the club infused her soul and for just a moment she let the music sway her just a little bit closer.

Memories of another night long ago flooded her senses and she released a pent-up sigh. How many centuries had she been wrapped up in chasing Persephone from the Underworld and back again?

Too many to think about.

She slid in close and tucked her hand in his. The animal musk of him invaded her senses as one palm skimmed down to her waist. She wanted him.

The idea was maddening. He was nothing like the men she took to her bed a millennium ago.

There. She admitted it to herself. She did want to sleep with the arrogant ass.

He made her feel safe but stirred her pulse at the same time.

The music pulsed; the electronica jingle bell beat morphing into a slow song. Lights dimmed and Nick pulled her close. His erection pressed against her stomach and she moaned as his lips claimed hers for another panty soaking kiss.

"Come with me," he murmured against her lips, tugging her into a hidden alcove. Behind him, a door opened, revealing a small storeroom filled with excess tables and chairs.

"How did you know this was here?"

"Perks of the job. Let's just say Hades values my services."

"What kind of services?"

His eyes gleamed bright and for a moment Demi could see something other than human shimmering in his gaze. "Do really want me to answer that?"

Desire and fear skittered along her spine. "I wouldn't have asked you if I didn't want to know, now would I?"

Nick smiled, his eyes picking up an animalistic glow. "Let's just say, I know how to make sure people stay well behaved."

"You really were indentured to him, then?"

"I was, indeed." His response was

bitter.

"But now you've found love so you get your armor back, is that it?"

Nick blinked, a surprised laugh erupting from his lips. "You really get down to brass tacks, don't you?"

"Something like that." Demi grinned. This was going to be fun. She reached underneath her skirt and hooked the scandalously thin pair of cherry-colored panties with her thumbs and slid them over her hips.

She wanted him now. The liquid heat between her thighs demanded release.

"Well, well. Ms. Demi, you are a

sugary bit of cake after all."

"Do you want a taste to find out?"

She dropped the panties on the floor and moved into his embrace, his lips sealing hers in a kiss.

"Oh, yes," he whispered as he pulled his mouth from hers, his voice hoarse with need. "I want to bury myself in that sweetness until we're both singing. How does that sound?"

She fumbled with the unfamiliar fastenings of his leathers for a moment, and then at last his cock sprang free.

His hand covered hers and her gaze snapped up to meet his.

"If we do this, it's not casual. Not for me." His voice was throaty and she wanted nothing more than to drown in every part of him.

"I know," she whispered.

Demi slid her hands down his cock. The tip was already seeping his desire and she bent down to lick it, eliciting a moan.

This wasn't just a one-night stand. Even as she moved against him, she knew it in her bones.

Demi shifted in his arms. She lifted her mesh skirt, her backside brushing against his erection. Bracing herself against the wall, she thrust her ass in the air and glanced over her shoulder. "Now. Take me now."

Eyes glowing shifter fire, Nick moved against her, the tip of him teasing her pussy. He slid in and Demi gasped as his thickness filled her empty places.

"Goddess," she hissed as he reached around her and pinched her nipples through the bustier, sending little fissions of fire right to the center of her being.

"That you are."

If only he knew.

But that was a conversation for another time.

He gripped her hips and began to pump in and out of her with precision. Every movement stretching her wider than she ever thought possible.

Demi panted, her nipples tiny pebbles under the club wear. What she wouldn't give to have this man wrapped in her sheets, pleasuring her with more than a fuck against a wall.

As he moved against her, his hand moving between them to flick her clit, she clung to him, her body on fire. Some nights were meant to last and this one would. She came, riding his cock and screaming her release.

Something sharp grazed her neck and she felt his teeth as they pierced her flesh, his fierce thrusting bringing pleasure and pain together in a fusion of sensation that made her eyes almost roll back in her head.

Her knees gave way and he caught her as the last of his passion rocked them. Nick held her close as her body convulsed around his once more. Then, they both rested propped up against the wall until their breathing slowed.

"You okay?" He smoothed sweat dampened hair from her temple and brushed a kiss across her forehead. Her Santa hat was long gone, her dark hair a tousled mess around her shoulders.

Demi didn't want to move. The moment was perfect. He was still inside her.

"Yes." Her reply was shaky. "I really am."

He withdrew from her and before she could murmur a response, he was holding out her discarded pair of panties with a quirky smile on his face. His liquid eyes glowed in the dim room.

Nick chuckled. "Your panties, my lady."

"Thanks." Demi stepped into them and met his amused glance with a kiss. "I don't know about you, but I'm not ready for this night to be over."

"Neither am I."

"Come on. I know this great little coffee shop that serves amazing lattes." He pressed a kiss to her lips and wrapped an arm around her shoulders, ushering her back out into the holiday techno beat and the wild lights of the club.

A smile curved over Demi's lips. "I can hardly wait."

They strolled through the door and out into the night air. The line for entrance into the club had grown with more holiday revelers since they were inside.

Nick offered her his arm. "Did you find whoever it was you were looking for in there?"

Demi paused. "You know, I think

I did."

"That girl looks an awful lot like you. You should be proud." Nick glanced back toward the sea of writhing bodies. "And Hades? He deserved that and more."

"You know, I think I like you, Nick. Let's go try one of those lattes."

Nick tugged her against his muscular chest. "Your wish is my command."

She watched a lock of white hair fall across his eyes and noticed, not for the first time, the very sexy cleft in his chin and the way he always seemed to pay attention to her every word.

This was something new.

Demi allowed herself to bask in his warmth. Nick's commanding air of self-confidence was, in itself, refreshing. This man would be no pushover and, well, she could get used to that.

"He really did look good with a collar and leash, didn't he?" Demi mused.

"You should see them on weeknights. She makes him into an end table while she watches *Extreme Bachelor*."

Laughter trickled out and soon she reveled in the feeling. Her daughter was more than capable of handling an oaf like Hades.

As she stepped in the dead grass, flowers bloomed. "Life, love, and cupcakes." She snorted as a particularly persistent night blooming flower brushed her ankle in thanks. It was time for her, now.

A pomegranate lay abandoned in the grass and she considered it for the briefest of moments. Her foot swung forward in a kick, sending it careening into the darkness beyond. *Take that, Hades, you miserable son of a bitch.*

"Let's go check out that coffee shop. Then we can go to my place." Demi planted a kiss on Nick's arm. "I have an idea what we can do with some triple chocolate frosting, a sprig of mistletoe, and a really long roll of red ribbon."

"Oh, woman. I do like the way you think."

"You know, I always did have a thing for polar bears." Demi mused.

She wasn't sure where this was going to lead, but maybe a goddess and a tarnished armored bear could find happiness.

The holidays were a time for miracles and it was time she had one just for her. Her arm tightened around Nick and she laid her head against his shoulder. But there was one thing she wondered about.

"So, are you going to tell me how you ended up under Charon's thumb?" She asked, loving the eye roll she got as a response.

"Oh, Cupcake. Really?"

"Yup."

"Wait till we get to the coffee shop. This might take a while."

Demi giggled. Goddess, but she hoped so. She really, really did.

For more of Mistle Tie Me, please visit your favorite online retailer.

MORE FROM GINA KINCADE

Silver Circle Witches

Red Moon Rising

Shadow Legacies

Hunter Moon

Ghost Moon

Blood Moon

Coming Soon!

Born of Hellfire

Hellbound Heart

Demon's Playground

Devil's Mate

Coming Soon!

Shifting Hearts Dating App

Mistle Tie Me

Bear It All

Chocolate Moon Cafe

Your Wolfish Heart

Outfoxing Her Mate

Shifting Hearts Dating Agency

One True Mate: Furever Shifter
Mates, Book 2

His Furever Mate: Furever Shifter
Mates, Book 3

Coming Soon!

Green Rock Falls

Accidentally Forever

Single Titles

What Lies Within Us

A Modern Day Witch Hunt

When the Snow Flies

CONNECT WITH GINA

Facebook

https://www.facebook.com/authorg

inakincade/

Newsletter Mailing List

https://landing.mailerlite.com/webf

orms/landing/r1r5n4

Twitter

https://twitter.com/ginakincade

BookBub

https://www.bookbub.com/authors /gina-kincade

Blog

https://themistressjournals.blogspo t.com/

Booksprout

https://booksprout.co/author/422 9/gina-kincade

Instagram

https://www.instagram.com/ginaki ncade/

Goodreads

https://www.goodreads.com/author /show/4806016.Gina_Kincade

ABOUT GINA KINCADE

USA Today Bestselling Author Gina Kincade has been penning romance since she was seventeen years old. She writes to a diverse range of genres where vampires and were-creatures will rip out a villainous heart without thinking twice, or bodyguards and heroic cowboys will obliterate miscreants, and then finally celebrate winning by engaging in steamy romances forged in fictional worlds readers yearn to crawl into.

A busy mom to three children, she lives in her wild household of two rambunctious dogs, a devoted, loving cat who believes herself to be royalty, and twelve crazy little chickens. She loves healthy home cooking, gardening, warm beaches, fast cars, and horseback riding.

Gina is also the C.E.O of Naughty Nights Press LLC, a quality publisher of contemporary romance, paranormal fiction, and sensual erotica.

Ms. Kincade's life is full, time is never on her side, and she wouldn't change a moment of it!